A Journey Through the Night

For-
Neil and Ellen -
With love + prayers -

By

Dawn L. Carey
with
Betty Robison

Dawn L. Carey

xulon
PRESS

Rob and Dylan

Chapter One

*"...I will strengthen you, I will help you,
I will uphold you..."* Isaiah 41:10

*The sound of a car in the drive was for a moment reassuring.
Surely it must be Rob.*

My husband, Rob, had gone with friends to a retirement party for a co-worker. I'd had a busy day and was glad to stay home and go to bed early. Rob didn't stay out late unless we were together.

At one o'clock in the morning I awakened to discover that Rob was not home yet. I got up and went into the bathroom. Suddenly my heart began to pound wildly. I became shaky and thought I might faint. I had never experienced anything like this before.

After getting a drink of water, I went back to bed, and lay there, wide-awake, sensing that something was not right. At the sound of the car outside, I rolled over in bed and, with a mixture of fear and hope, told myself, "He's home." The hope was short-lived as I recognized the sound, also, of a police radio.

As I got out of bed and put on my robe, the doorbell rang. I glanced at the clock. Two o'clock in the morning.

The sheriff's deputy at the door asked, "Are you Mrs. Rasmussen?" When I replied, "Yes, I am," he asked if he could come in. I reached out, took his hand, and said, "Just tell me if he is dead." I already knew.

He came inside and insisted that I be seated. We sat on the couch and I said again, "Just tell me if he is dead." He answered, "Yes, he is."

The shock against which I had been struggling took over. I began shaking. The deputy asked if there was anyone he could call, and I asked him to telephone my parents. I heard him at the kitchen phone telling them, "I'm at your daughter's house. She is O.K. but there has been an accident and I think you should come."

I recovered my senses enough to ask him to call Rob's brother, Mike, who lived nearby. In the numbness of shock, my only reaction was the physical trembling. My mind, my emotions, were all temporarily at a standstill.

But as Mike walked through the door, I screamed, "Oh God, he's dead." With a great swell, the sobbing began. After the crying subsided somewhat, I sat with my folks, Mike, and the deputy as we tried to fit together what had happened.

Rob was returning from the retirement party. He had dropped our friend, Shelby, off at his house. He had come to a short bend in the road and, as nearly as the officers could tell from skid marks, he had swerved to miss something in the road. In coming back, he had overcorrected and the Toyota Land cruiser flipped on its side. The removable top, which Rob had planned to replace with another, was not firmly fixed, and came off. Rob flew out, striking his head. The officer said he had died within a minute from massive head injuries.

Though they took him by ambulance to the hospital, he was pronounced dead on arrival. The sheriff had come immediately to notify me.

At the exact time I had awakened and experienced the wildly pounding heart, the accident had occurred.

While we were talking, our son, Dylan, woke and came out into the living room. He looked sleepily around the room and asked, "What's wrong?" My own state of shock and my natural instinct as a mother to protect him must have prompted me to say, "It's O.K., go back to bed." Somehow, I didn't want him to hear anything bad in the middle of the night.

There are always things in life we would like to do differently if we could. Dylan was an obedient child and he went back to bed.

But he knew it wasn't really O.K. I learned later that he lay awake straining to hear all that was said. He lay there and cried. I cry to think about it now.

When I first became a Christian, I had thought that my life was too good. I had a vague fear that God might do something to test my faith and see how committed I was. Yet from the time the sheriff came to my door and told me Rob was dead, I forgot all about my fatalistic fears. I did not think, "Here it is. I knew it was going to happen." I did not think, either, that this was something God did to me to test my faith. I had an assurance from the first that God in His great wisdom had known about it and had in many ways been preparing me for it.

I was grateful for the scripture I had memorized in the two years between my conversion and Rob's death. God's word began to minister to me right away. I found myself repeating over and over the words of Isaiah 41.10: *"Fear not, for I am with you, be not dismayed for I am your God; I will strengthen you, I will help you, I will uphold you with my victorious right hand."* I found that just repeating the words was soothing. The meaning penetrated in time.

There were many other passages from the Bible that calmed my heart and provided strength in my times of weakness. God, Himself, was comforting me in a way no one else could.

Even though the comfort is always there when we are alone with God, He knows we also need people. He made us social creatures. So many people were there as I began to stumble my way through the steps of grief. Each day brought a new need—and a new provision.

At first, my main concern was that I didn't know where Rob was. Had he become a Christian quietly sometime? He wasn't the type of person to verbalize such things easily. Would I ever see him again? I felt I had to know.

The pastor of our church came to the house to offer help. He saw my agitated state was tearing me apart. I wanted so much to know Rob was in heaven. That dear pastor would have offered any solace he thought would help. I knew, however, he would never sacrifice integrity and his understanding of the truth to spare my feelings. I appreciated that. "Dawn," he said, "there is nothing you can do now except trust God." The simplicity of that statement somehow gave my thinking a new focus. It was no longer an absolute necessity that I know. It was enough that God knew. My part was to hope and trust and leave it with the Lord.

I still wonder sometimes, but I have learned to accept the fact that if God had wanted me to know, He would have arranged it. I hope Rob at some time in his quiet way said, "Yes, Lord, I believe you died for me, and I accept you as my Savior." If he did, then I will see him again. If he didn't, then I won't. That hurts, but it is the truth. God's Word says so.

* * * * * * *

Chapter Two

"Peace I leave with you; my peace I give to you;
not as the world gives, do I give to you..
Let not your heart be troubled, nor let it be fearful."
John 14:27

*T*he days following Rob's death were difficult.

How can we say goodbye to someone we love without experiencing pain? The answer is obvious. We can't. Suffering is a necessary part of grief. But along with the suffering comes a flood of memories. Bittersweet and beautiful therapy. How grateful I was for the memories. I often recalled in those days every small detail of Rob's proposal and our marriage.

At that time I was not a Christian, I was a divorcee and I had a baby son. My life was without much direction except to care for my son, Dylan. When Dylan was less than a year old, Rob Rasmussen asked me to go to Magic Mountain, a Southern California amusement park. I didn't think of it as a date because Rob was the "boy down the block" I'd known since we were children. My Dad had taken us both fishing and boating, taught us to shoot, and often took Rob on hunting trips. I thought of Rob as a dependable friend who was always there, very much as a brother would be. I knew he felt I should get out more, so I agreed to go.

When we got to Magic Mountain we sat at a table drinking a

soda. Neither of us was interested in the rides. We soon discovered that we both needed to talk. I talked about my broken marriage and some of the unhappy experiences. Rob talked of the time he spent in Vietnam and how it had affected him. We sat there for hours. As we talked I began to see Rob in a different way. He wasn't just the kid I had grown up with. Somewhere along the way he'd become a man. A man whose company I very much enjoyed.

After that evening we began going out. We were comfortable being together. The friendship we had always had was still there but something more seemed to be developing. I didn't know what to call it at first. When he went to Arizona to take a job there, I couldn't believe how much I missed him. He wrote me almost every day. When he called me one weekend, I told him, "I think I love you." He said, "Well, I know I love you. I have loved you for a long time." Much later he shared with me that when Andy and I had married he was very upset. He told his mother, "I'll never find anyone like Dawn." It is to Rob's credit that he remained a good friend both to Andy and to me during that marriage. I had never suspected he cared for me in any way other than as a friend.

Rob didn't stay in Arizona. He came back to Southern California and enrolled in Los Angeles Trade Tech School to become a licensed electrician. We decided to get married and I would work while he went to school.

There was none of the fanfare of my first wedding. There were about twenty-five friends and family members in attendance. We were incredibly happy.

Dylan, who was then two, had no problem adjusting to having Rob for a dad. They were already good friends. It wasn't difficult becoming a family. Rob and I were very much in love. Dylan loved us both. With school, work, family and friends, the days were full. Most of the married couples of our acquaintance were friends we had known in high school.

We were a part of a smaller circle of four couples, a warm, loving group, which was especially close. There were Bev and Shelby, Dixie and John, Chris and Wayne, along with Rob and me. The eight of us were compatible friends and enjoyed the times we could all be together.

My friend, Dixie, had always been a very special person in my eyes. I knew in high school that she went to church faithfully and called herself a "Christian." I didn't know what that meant, but it seemed to add somewhat to her specialness. I treasured her friendship. We both had sons and could talk mother-to-mother, comparing growth behavior patterns and our plans for the future of our boys.

Our friend, Chris, was as interested in going to church as Dixie. The fourth in our circle of housewives, who had been schoolmates, was Bev. Dixie and Chris took Bev to Bible Study Fellowship where she "accepted the Lord," they told me. I didn't know what they meant by that but wasn't greatly disturbed by it.

Our relationship as a close circle of old friends hadn't changed, and no one was bugging me to make any changes or to become a "fanatic." That is, until one day when Bev called me with a strange message. I was in the kitchen washing dishes when the telephone rang. I had been feeling very content and happy with life in general. I was thinking, "I must have the most wonderful, considerate, loving husband in the world." Dylan, our son, was a good-natured, intelligent little boy. When Rob finished school he would likely provide well for us. The only very slight shadow was the fact that I hadn't gotten pregnant and Rob and I very much wanted Dylan to have brothers and sisters.

I answered the phone. "Dawn," Bev began in a slightly nervous tone, "I love you and I don't want you to go to hell. But you are." I was stunned. What was she talking about? I thought she must have gone off the deep end and didn't know what she was saying. All I could say was, "Why?" I had never done anything really bad. I didn't see why anyone, and I of all people, should have to go to hell. Wasn't that for people who commit murder and all those things people get arrested for?

Nothing seemed to click. Why was Bev pouring all this "religious stuff" on me? I couldn't help being angry with her. After that the friendship was somewhat strained. I couldn't forget what she had said. Also, there were recurring, nagging questions I kept asking myself, "What if she's right? What if I am supposed to do something and don't do it? And something happens to me?" I felt strangely uneasy.

Shortly after that Chris called me one evening. I knew at once something was wrong. Chris and Wayne also had one child, a little girl, Jodie. "Dawn, will you watch Jodie for me? I have to go to the hospital." I asked what had happened and she explained.

It seems that afternoon while Dixie was working; the baby-sitter was driving with Dixie's twenty-two month old son, Jason. She hit a parked car and Jason had gone through the windshield. He suffered major head injuries and, at the hospital, Dixie was told he probably would not live through the night. Jason died the next morning and, when I heard it, I fell apart. The thought of losing a child was more than I could bear.

Dylan was so important to me. The difficulty I was having getting pregnant was probably due to the questionable DES drug my mother had taken to avoid miscarriage before I was born. It was beginning to look as if Dylan might be our only child. I knew I could never bear to lose him. As I thought about Dixie losing her son, I lost control of my emotions. What could I say to Dixie? I didn't want to go see her. I didn't want to attend the funeral, but knew I must.

At the funeral I sat and cried uncontrollably the whole time. Dixie hugged and patted me. She kept saying, "Don't worry. Everything is O.K. Jason is with the Lord and I will see him again." I could not get hold of the meaning of her words. But her quiet calm helped calm me.

In the days following I saw Dixie suffer as any mother would suffer. She grieved for her loss and missed Jason desperately. She said often that she wished she could just hold him again. Yet, through it all, she had a serenity that I couldn't begin to understand.

I didn't know it then but I was watching her faith at work and it was doing something to me. I couldn't believe it was possible to have so much peace at a time like that. I realized she had something I didn't know anything about and I wanted to know more about it.

* * * * * * * *

Chapter Three

"These things I remember; and I pour out my soul within me."
Psalm 42:4

*A*fter Rob's death, the memories came and went.

They couldn't fill the desperate hurting void, but they were there to help each day pass. I didn't want to be with people much. The first few days I just sat and stared out the window. I resented the people driving by. They were going to work, going shopping, going out to lunch. They were laughing and talking as though nothing had happened. Life went on. Business as usual. Didn't they know my world was crumbling?

I was growing more and more inward. Remembering the past was much easier than facing the future. Or the present. I thought of the many plans we had made, as Rob was finishing school. Before he finished school, we discussed the advantages of moving to a small town, possibly in Oregon or Northern California. We liked the mountains and enjoyed the outdoors. Getting away from the big city would be a better way to raise Dylan. So every time we had a few extra days we drove up the coast, searching for the dream place. After three or four such trips as far north as Oregon and back down through Northern California, we stopped at a small town called "Paradise." Our next-door neighbor had suggested we visit this place. It promised to be just the quiet, smog-free area we were seeking. The tree-lined streets seemed to say, "welcome."

In the spring when Rob graduated, we visited Paradise once more to be certain. With dogwood and lilacs in bloom, it was even more inviting than we remembered. We knew this was where we wanted to make our home, to bring up our son. As we drove to Southern California, we sensed we were about to embark on an exciting future. Rob could be an electrician one place as well as another. We had saved enough money to pay rent and buy groceries for a while. So we weren't worried about anything—just eager to begin living in Paradise.

When we went back to Los Angeles to prepare for the move, we found our friends had planned a large "going away" party. They gave us so many gifts and "best wishes" we wondered briefly if we should leave. I received a gift from our friend Chris that caused me once again to recall Bev's telephone call. The gift was a Living Bible, the Bible in modern language. I had never owned a Bible, never read or been interested in looking at one before. But receiving a Bible of my own stirred within me a desire to read it. For the first time in my life I wanted to know what was in it. Thoughts kept coming into my mind. "Bev, Dixie and Chris seem to have something in common I don't share. What is it?" Perhaps I could find some answers that would explain Dixie's quiet faith. Or why Bev had felt she must speak so sternly to me at one time. Bev and I were still friends and I had concluded she might not have meant what she said. We all do impetuous things sometimes. I would not hold it against her. I did determine to read this Book as soon as I had time. That time came much later.

Meanwhile, we packed all our things and prepared to leave. Shelby and Bev, who had also decided to relocate to Paradise, proved to be the best of friends. They rented a U-Haul truck in Paradise, drove it to Southern California, and helped us move north. They had (also) found a duplex for us, and when we arrived all the utilities were connected and ready to go. All we had to do was unload the furniture and settle in. From the first, it felt like home.

Rob soon got a job with an electrical company. Dylan made friends easily. I busied myself with unpacking; hanging pictures and doing all the little things that go into making a house a home.

This truly was a little bit of Paradise.

We adjusted quickly to small town life. Dixie and John chose to move to Paradise a few months after we did. Chris and Wayne came north also, but settled near Lake Tahoe. So the four couples that had been friends since high school were often together again. I loved the sense of continuity it provided.

My parents came to visit and also fell in love with the area. Dad felt it was time to retire and transferred his part of his sporting goods store in Sunland to my brother, Dick. After visiting several other prospective retirement areas, Mom and Dad made the decision to move to Paradise.

Surrounded by family and friends, I was enveloped in a false sense of security. Life would always be like this.

* * * * * * *

Chapter Four

"...My grace is sufficient for you,
for power is perfected in weakness..."
II Corinthians 12:9

*F*or days after Rob's accident I did what I thought a Christian was suppose to do.

I bore up bravely. No one saw me cry. No one, except on occasions, Dylan. When he sensed I was suffering, he stood behind my chair and patted me on the shoulder. He didn't say anything. Just stood there patting me.

Self-pity came and went. I managed to cover any signs of anger and frustration most of the time. I tried not to let anyone see my sorrow. I had the mistaken idea that a Christian should be silent, staunch, accepting. I hadn't been a Christian long enough to drop some early misconceptions. After three months of trying to act like everything was fine, my nerves were taut and ready to snap.

One night, after tossing sleeplessly for hours, all my pent-up feeling broke loose. I shouted at the top of my lungs, "Oh God, why?" I felt out of control. Anger flooded over me and I continued to scream, "Why?" Soon I began to experience a strong sense of release. So many feelings were buried inside me—feelings that no one can live with for long. I hadn't recognized or acknowledged that there was anything in me that was less than beautiful. Because I was immature in the Christian faith I was trying to live out a preconceived notion of how one should meet adversity.

I thought I had no right to be angry. Now, suddenly, I realized there was much anger within me. I had to face facts. Not until I acknowledged and released the anger deep within me did I truly begin the necessary grief process.

I had already experienced the early numbness and shock. The important paperwork and the people around me had sustained me for a while. Now, that sustenance was gone and reality had set in. I would pray, "God make me brave. Make me strong." And it didn't help. I wasn't brave. I wasn't strong, I didn't doubt for a moment that God had those qualities and wanted to impart them to me. There is a verse that speaks about my weakness (II Corinthians 12; 9) and God's power. I had to stop trying to dredge up my own strength. It wasn't there. But God's power was available to me. That realization helped.

God's promises were beginning to be very precious to me. I knew He could meet any situation I might find myself in, including the loss of my husband and the subsequent anger I was experiencing. But before I could appropriate God's power I had to find out what was blocking my reception of it. I began looking at facts squarely, sorting out my feelings. I discovered, to my dismay, that I was angry with Rob for going out that evening. I found myself saying, "Why didn't you just stay home? Why did you have to go?"

In my mind, I played around with that "why" and "what if" for several days. And one night I realized I had to forgive him. Of course I couldn't look him in the eye and say, "I forgive you." Yet, I knew I was never to proceed with healing from this loss until I forgave him. I knew, somehow, the accident was not his fault and he had not gone out deliberately to die that night. For my part, though, the anger was there and I needed to forgive him. So I verbalized it, "I forgive you." Just as though he were there. The anger began to subside and eventually disappeared.

The next stage of healing was depression. Strange that it should be a part of the process of healing, but I had it and I understand most people do to some degree. Depression is not usually a part of my make-up. Mine came and went at intervals. Sometimes prayer and sheer willpower overcame it. Other times it settled on and in me until nothing I could do would help. At times like that I needed to draw on God's power and resources until I came out of it. It helped to recall my conversion and what had happened in my life as a result of it.

I recalled those incidents that had led up to my decision to give my life to Christ. There had been in my childhood the death of a neighbor girl killed on a bicycle. I had wondered as a child if that girl was gone forever or was there somewhere that good people go after they die. Then much later after I was grown, the death of Dixie's son, Jason. It has been so devastating to me, but Dixie had a strong assurance she would see this son again. Before that, of course, had been Bev's telephone call that had unnerved me for a while. How dare she say I was going to hell? I wasn't even convinced there was such a place. The next occasion when God succeeded in getting my attention was when Chris gave me a Bible as a going away present. She must have put great store in this Book to want me to have one.

After we moved to Paradise I forgot all about that Bible until one day when Bev and I were chatting over a cup of tea. She told me about a Bible study she was attending in the nearby town of Chico. She invited me to go with her. I thought about my new Bible and how it hadn't made much sense the few times I had attempted to read it. Going to a study class might be the answer to helping me understand what the Bible was saying. I agreed to go. Though I didn't say so, I was still not convinced there was anything wrong with me. Bev had to be a little mixed up on that score. I did want to find out what it meant to be a Christian. Dixie had made such an impact on my life that I hoped to know more of the things she knew.

The Bible class proved to be just what I needed. The women were open and friendly, many of them young mothers like myself. All of our discussions centered on the scripture and how it applied to our lives today. I was soon to learn that there was more than just becoming acquainted with what the Bible says. God was waiting for me to make a commitment to Him and His plan for me before the scripture could have relevant meaning so I could apply its truths to my situation.

* * * * * * *

Chapter Five

*"And this I pray, that your love may abound still more
and more in real knowledge and all discernment..."*
Philippians 1:9

*I*n those days before my conversion, I began to see things that
startled me.

While attending Bible class with Bev, I read in the book of
Romans, "all have sinned and come short of God's requirements."
In that same book of the Bible there was a statement that there is
not one person who is right in God's sight.

Grasping those truths, I realized for the first time that I was
included in the category of all sinners. I had been telling myself for
so long that I wasn't a sinner. There wasn't any reason for me to go
to hell. Hadn't I tried all my life to be good? But now, God was
saying, "You, Dawn Rasmussen, are a sinner." That came into my
heart from God's word, the Bible. I couldn't any longer be angry
with Bev.

One evening after Bible study I picked up a paperback book
written by a man named H. S. Vigeveno. The title of the book was
"Is It Real?" Someone had given it to me and I had never taken the
time to read it. Now the title seemed to beckon me. I read the book
from cover to cover. The author gave logical answers to many questions posed by the world's skeptics. I became totally engrossed in

the book and found myself agreeing with the conclusions contained there. The author explained how none of us live up to God's standards. We are all condemned to die for our sins. God's provision for us is Jesus Christ who took the penalty on himself and died in our place. All we have to do is believe that and receive the pardon God offers. Then we begin to live for Him.

At the end of the book there was a printed prayer that the author suggested I pray. I prayed it and waited. Nothing happened, so I went to bed.

The next day when Bev and I were talking I mentioned the book. I said, "I prayed that prayer last night."

Bev looked perplexed, "What prayer?"

"The one in the book." And I showed it to her.

The prayer began, "Heavenly Father, if you are really there..." I told Bev I had prayed the prayer word for word and told God I was willing to come to Him and receive His forgiveness for my sins.

Bev was obviously trying to contain her excitement as she asked, "Did you really mean it?"

"Yes," I said, " I really did. But what do I do now? Isn't there something else I have to do?"

"No," Bev replied, "you've done it. God did the rest."

At that moment I sensed within myself a filling up. The void, which had been waiting for Christ, was now filled with Him. At last, I found what I had been searching for all my life. And, though I wasn't aware of it at the time, the prayers of Bev, Chris and Dixie had just been answered.

As a family, there wasn't much change in our life-style after my conversion. I began taking Dylan to Sunday school and sometimes staying for church. Rob didn't see church as a high priority so he often made other plans for our Sundays. I went along with his plans because I loved him too much to cause any dissension between us. Rob didn't mind if I went to church if there wasn't anything else to do.

Bev and I continued to attend the Bible studies in Chico. Being a Christian was so new to me that I really wasn't sure what I should be doing about it. I was learning principles from the Bible and how to apply them daily to my life. The real conflict going on in me was a fear that I might change so much that Rob would not continue loving me. He thought I was great the way I was when he married me. I didn't want anything to ruin our marriage.

Nevertheless, I felt drawn two ways. I knew there were areas in my personality that needed changing in God's eyes. Yet I didn't want Rob to see anything different in the woman he had loved all along. I sometimes felt I was living in two worlds.

* * * * * * * *

Chapter Six

"For I am confident of this very thing, that He who began a good work in you will perfect it until the day of Christ Jesus."
Philippians 1:6

I would never have admitted to Rob that I was being torn two ways.

After Rob's death I kept remembering all the incidents that pertained to my being a Christian. I tried to recall everything Rob had said, how he had reacted. I guess I was trying to convince myself he really had at some time also made a personal commitment to Christ. I remembered that he went to church with us once in a while and always attended Dylan's Sunday school programs and events.

Rob and Dylan were as close as any father and son could be. Though Dylan knew that Rob was his stepfather and Andy was his father, he never saw Andy. It was easy for him to consider Rob his "Daddy." As for Rob, he was as proud of Dylan as if he were his own. There was a very strong bond between the two.

One day when Dylan was six years old, he came home from Awana's, a church boys and girls club, and told us that he had asked Jesus into his heart. Rob listened with interest, but didn't comment.

There had never been any arguments about my being a Christian or attending church. We just didn't discuss it much because Rob didn't understand what I was experiencing. He was generous and fair and was probably struggling to sort things out in his own ways.

Rob's parents visited us one Easter. With his brother and sister-in-law, we all attended church. Rob was always in favor of attending church on Christmas and Easter. I think he believed it was the American thing to do. The message that day was an especially powerful one. The pastor spoke of salvation, why Jesus Christ had to die and be resurrected the third day. All because of you and me so that we could be saved from God's judgment on our sins.

After that day, Rob began asking questions. What did it mean to be "saved?" I told him that the Bible teaches that we are all sinners and God sent Jesus Christ to die for us. God's judgment would be on anyone who didn't accept what Christ had done. I told Rob that he had to make that commitment to be right with God. If anything happened to him and he hadn't done that he would go to hell. I certainly didn't want that. Rob was a quiet, thoughtful person and I knew he was weighing my answer. He did not become angry as I had when Bev had first confronted me about the same truth. Rob's reaction was simply to become very quiet. Every week or so he would ask me another question. I answered as best I knew how and prayed God would make it real to him and he would respond. Perhaps he did. I could only hope. It was something only God knew for certain now.

I knew I had to get on with living. As a mother, it was important that I do all I could to restore my son's world to normalcy. The few times I cried in front of him, Dylan just stood and patted me. Sometimes he said, "I love you, Mom." We talked often about how God doesn't make mistakes and Dylan seemed to accept our loss more readily than I. His faith was so perfect for one so young. I worried sometimes that he was not grieving and didn't seem upset. I know now that he was coping in a different way. His frustrations were demonstrated in ways other than tears.

His teacher said that Dylan was being a poor sport on the school ground. He must have been thinking, "I can't catch that ball. I can't win this game. I can't even have a father." While he never expressed these thoughts to me, I believe now that was what was happening. I know he was bothered when I didn't feel well. I often had severe headaches and he became frightened. He was afraid I, too, might die. That seemed to be his only fear.

Most of the time Dylan was cheerful and my chief encourager. He was always concerned for me. He often wrote comforting notes to me. One I have tucked away in my memorabilia box is covered with hand-drawn hearts. It reads, "Dear Mom, I love you. I am sorry about Daddy. Love, Dylan."

Dylan's most difficult time was perhaps immediately after Rob's death. He had a grown-up decision to make and, being just a boy, didn't know how to make it. He was visibly upset. The day after Rob died I noticed Dylan whispering to his grandparents and to his Uncle Mike something he was obviously trying to keep from me. On Christmas Eve I was to discover what it was.

* * * * * * *

Chapter Seven

*"Oh let those who fear the Lord say,
'His lovingkindness is everlasting."*
Psalm 118:4

I dreaded the holidays.

As a family all our holidays had been fun. Fourth of July fireworks and picnics, Halloween costumes, overeating on Thanksgiving, excitement of Christmas and birthday parties, dressing up for Easter. We did it all as a family. It had seemed the pattern was permanent and we were snugly certain it would go on forever. Now, all that was changed.

I couldn't imagine enjoying Christmas without Rob. For Dylan's sake, I knew I had to make the effort. The day after Rob's death our friends, Shelby, John and Wayne had bought a Christmas tree and brought it to our house. They wanted to be sure Dylan had one. So we had a tree to decorate.

The day Rob died was Saturday and I had to work. Dylan and Rob were acting very secretive at breakfast. They seemed to have plans for the day that they didn't want to share with me. I suspected it might have something to do with Christmas although that was unlikely. Rob was a last-minute Christmas shopper and this was only December 8.

I didn't think much about it that evening. Chris and Wayne had come over from Tahoe and the eight of us went out to dinner. The friendly banter and teasing between old friends made the dinner that evening especially pleasant. We were comfortable being together again. It seemed we had always known one another.

We women shared a faith that made us even closer friends now than in the past. I had finally discovered where Dixie had received her calm serenity in the face of tragedy. Though I didn't think I could ever be like Dixie, it was a joy to know that the same God who had supplied her strength was now my God, too. What a peaceful thought.

After dinner we had all gone to our home to enjoy the rest of the evening. As we sat talking, John mentioned that a friend who worked with him at the telephone company was retiring. There was a retirement party that evening and he felt he really should go. It was decided that the men would all go for a while, and leave the wives at home to talk. We never seemed to have enough time for that.

Eventually, after a pleasant interlude of reminiscing we agreed we were all getting tired. Bev said she should go home and get some sleep. Dixie and Chris left about the same time, and I had gone to bed.

That was over two weeks ago and now it was Christmas Eve. I didn't even want to think about Christmas, as I answered a knock at the door. There stood Mike, my brother-in-law, with Rob and Dylan's surprise. As I opened the door Mike struggled through, carrying a beautiful oak rocking chair. Dylan had tied a ribbon around it and pasted large bows here and there. Dylan's large brown eyes were bright with excitement as he watched for my reaction. Did I like it? I had to fight back the tears.

Rob and Dylan had bought the chair unfinished on that fateful Saturday. They had hidden it under the house intending to do the staining and varnishing secretly. Their plan was to surprise me with the rocking chair on Christmas day. I recalled how upset Dylan had seemed the day after Rob's death as he went from one adult to another whispering quietly. No one had known about the present except Rob and Dylan. And Dylan knew he had to do something about it. That was quite a responsibility for a seven-and-a-half year old boy who has just lost his father. He took care of the matter by getting his Uncle Mike to stain and finish the chair. Here it was in front of me, a gift from Dylan and Rob. I thought I had never seen anything so beautiful. All that love tied up in ribbon and bows. All that love directed my way.

"Thank you, Mike. Thank you, Dylan. Thank you, Rob."

"And thank you, God, for being here when I need you."

In the days that followed I sat in that chair a lot. I still do in the rare moments I have just simply to relax and think. Like most busy people today, I don't find as much time for the simple things as I might like. But each time I hurry past that chair, out the door, on my way to work, there is a gentle tug at my heart.

We frequently need to be reminded that God manifests His great love for us in many ways. The greatest, of course, was by giving His own beloved Son to die for us. But it doesn't stop there. Once we accept what He has done for us and begin to live for Him, He sends others to love us, and we can love in return. God's love never ends.

* * * * * * *

Chapter Eight

"Blessed be the Lord,
because He has heard the voice of my supplication."
Psalm 28:6

*I*t was strange, being called a widow.

I was too young. I knew many older women who were widows, but I couldn't relate to them. How could they know what I was experiencing? With my whole life before me? No husband and a son to bring up. It was a self-pity tool I employed often.

I have learned to look at life a bit differently now. Who is to say that grief is greater for some than for others? When we lose a loved one the void is there and it hurts. For someone who has been married forty or fifty years the hurt is heightened by multiplied memories. For one, like myself, young and married just a few years the hurt is deepened by unfulfilled dreams and plans that can never be completed.

But at the time I longed for someone who could identify with my hurt. God provided two such persons the first year-and-a-half after Rob's death. They have become my lifelong friends.

The first of these friends I met six weeks after Rob died. Susan, her husband and children had moved to Paradise a short time before. Our mothers were friends and felt we should get acquainted. So the two families got together one day and played Bingo. I was still in the earliest stages of widowhood. Wearing my brave exterior. Susan recalls the incident better than I and this is what she says.

> "My mother had told me about Dawn and I really didn't want to meet her. I wouldn't know what to say."

> "When we met I watched her, fascinated. How could anyone be acting so normal, smiling, talking, playing a game, when she has just lost her husband?"

> "I couldn't understand it. I knew if I had lost my husband, I would be ready for the 'funny farm.'"

After that, Susan came over to my house and brought her daughter, Leasa, who was Dylan's age. The two became instant friends and went into the backyard to explore its limits. We began to talk. Susan has confided since that she came, intending to stay only a few minutes, because she still felt a bit awkward. The few minutes stretched into three hours, and neither of us noticed the time. The rapport was instantaneous and we were comfortable sharing experiences. I was glad to find someone my own age that seemed to understand.

She said that several years before she had lost a three-year-old son and we discussed how much it hurts. She said she had not been able to talk about the loss to anyone. Bottled up inside her was a refusal to accept what had happened. She was trapped in a rut. She says she began thinking, "If she could accept losing her husband, then she must have something I don't have."

It was Susan's determination to discover what that secret ingredient was that brought about her conversion. In God's economy nothing is ever wasted. He began using my loss long before I had learned to deal with it myself. By combining my circumstances with someone else's prayers and witnessing he brought a whole family to Himself.

As our friendship developed, it seemed only natural to share with Susan where I was getting my strength. Susan said she had always believed in God but she didn't know there was anything personal involved. She wanted to know more about my personal relationship with Jesus Christ. I explained very simply that we are all born separated from God, and we have to do something about that. This is all we can do—believe that Jesus dies in our place and then ask Him to forgive us and come into our life. In doing this, we are no longer separated from God. We enter into a family relationship with Jesus our Lord, and God our Father.

I said, "I know it sounds simple. At one time it didn't make any sense to me at all. I thought I had to do something to earn acceptance by God. But I read in the Bible that there isn't anything I can do to get into God's family. All I can do is accept what He has already done. He instantly makes me His child."

Susan listened quietly and finally said, "What am I supposed to pray?" She had made her decision and soon her commitment was sealed as she asked Christ to come in and take control of her life. She was now one of God's spiritual children. Our bond of friendship grew stronger.

Susan was able, after so long a time, to accept the death of her little son, Ronnie. Now she could talk freely about it. God's healing had begun in her.

Through the witnessing of Susan's brother, Mike, Susan's husband, John, had been considering becoming a Christian. He made the commitment to Christ shortly after Susan did. They began, as a family, going to the church Dylan and I attended. Soon their daughters also became Christians.

Susan and I often sat with a cup of tea or coffee, talking over how we felt about life, in general. I remember how we concluded one day that we had both lost someone very dear to us, so now God wouldn't take anyone else from us. How foolish our philosophic meanderings when we take the path of our own wishes instead of being open to those things God allows.

The second special friend God provided was a young lady I met over a year later at the women's Bible study I attended. It was announced at the Bible study one day that Linnea from Alaska was visiting. Her husband, a U.S. Coast Guard helicopter pilot, had been killed two weeks before while on a rescue mission out of Kodiak. Linnea, the mother of two children, was six months pregnant with her third.

I sought out Linnea immediately after class. I introduced myself and told her I had lost my husband in an accident. I had not met anyone my own age that had lost a husband. I told her that if she ever needed to talk I was available.

We became friends and talked as often as we could. Linnea was in and out of town much of the time, still trying to make plans for a home for herself and her children. She thought she should go back to Cape Cod where she and her husband owned a home, but until the baby was born concluded she should stay near both sets of grandparents, who lived in California.

Our friendship developed quickly. Linnea needed someone who understood something of what she was going through. I was grateful for a friend who could sense what I had suffered. Our friendship was to mean even more a short time later when I would need her perhaps more than she needed me.

* * * * * * *

Chapter Nine

"God is our refuge and strength, a very present help in trouble."
Psalm 46:1

*O*ne day Dylan asked to be baptized.

I had never been baptized, and wasn't sure I wanted to go through that in front of everyone. But as I recalled how the Bible tells us that Jesus Christ, who never sinned, was baptized, I knew that we should follow His perfect example.

So, on Mother's Day, Dylan and I and two of Susan's daughters, Bonnie and Leasa, were baptized. The event made our families' friendship very special. During the baptismal ceremony, each of us was given an opportunity to share our spiritual experience. I said that I had accepted the Lord and I knew He would always take care of me and that He had a plan for my life. I added that when my husband was killed I learned to depend upon the Lord for everything. The children were asked, "Have you accepted Jesus into your heart and do you intend to live for Him from now on?" Dylan, always boisterous, answered with a loud "yes." That simple affirmation held a world of meaning for Dylan and for me.

Life was different without Rob. All my emotions and energies centered on Dylan. As a widow, with a dependent child, I collected Social Security. By planning and spending carefully I found it was not necessary for me to work full-time. I could be home when

Dylan was home from school. My part-time job with a tax consultant had flexible hours. It was ideal.

I took Dylan to school in the morning, went to work, and then picked him up on my way home. The arrangement was fine except when Dylan was sick. That is a problem which most working mothers face. Each solution depends on individual circumstances, of course. In my case, it was fortunate I had parents who were available and willing to baby-sit.

No matter how well a working mother has planned, though, it isn't easy. A part of you says, "My child needs me. No one else can fill my role." Another part says, "I have committed myself to this job. I must be responsible and be there when I say I will be there." A mother is torn two ways.

One particular school morning I was experiencing just such a struggle. Dylan had been ill with an ear infection and could not go to school. When I called the doctor, he told me to go by the pharmacy and pick up a prescription for eardrops. I promptly made arrangements to go by for the medication and take Dylan on to my parents before I went to work.

After getting the prescription at the pharmacy, I thought that to save time I would put the drops in Dylan's ears there in the car. Then we would proceed to Grandma's. As I put the drops in one ear, the immediate result was startling. Dylan, usually so cooperative, gave a blood-curdling scream. The medication must have burned the sensitive ear dreadfully. He continued screaming. I felt totally helpless. I was overwhelmed with a sense of guilt and inadequacy. I began to sob. Dylan was screaming. I was crying. It seemed we had been sitting there like that a long time when, suddenly, Dylan stopped screaming and looked up. He shouted, "Jesus, help us?" We both became calm and were able to get on with the day.

I'll never forget how Dylan was the one who realized first that the Lord could help. His faith always amazed me. His faith often helped strengthen mine. Yet, in spite of his strength and maturity beyond his years, I was often overprotective.

When Dylan was in the third grade, some of the children were riding bicycles to school. I thought that he was much too young and always said "no" when he asked if he could.

In many ways, because I had to be both mother and father, I said "no" too often simply to shield him from harm. I knew this tendency was not healthy and tried to guard against it. But there was always this thought in the back of my mind. "Dylan, you are all I have, and I alone am responsible for you. I can't afford to make mistakes." When I analyze the precautions now, I know they were prompted by a selfish desire to hold on to what was mine.

* * * * * * *

Chapter Ten

" Thine eyes have seen my unformed substance;
And in Thy book they were all written, the days that were
ordained for me, when as yet there was not one of them."
Psalm 139:16

I *thought about how much I relied on Dylan to fulfill my hopes and*
dreams.

Even the conception of that child was a vain effort on my part to save a hopeless marriage. In those days I didn't have God's Word for direction. I could only try to reason with my own frail human logic.

I'd married Andy because I was restless and didn't see my life going anywhere. I wanted to leave my parents' home and be "independent." Andy was a high school acquaintance who was in the Army stationed in Germany. When he came home on leave he asked for a date. After a whirlwind romance we decided to get married. I know I was more in love with the idea of going to Germany and having a place of my own than I was with Andy.

After a year the assignment in Germany was finished. I was on my way back to Southern California, six weeks before Andy would be returning on a military plane. I sat by a window, looking at the Atlantic Ocean below. There was plenty of time for thinking. Some of the youthful restlessness returned. What was the matter with me?

I had gotten away from my childhood home, been independent—as much as an Army wife can be. Yet, there was an emptiness that I couldn't explain.

Marriage wasn't the answer to everything as I had expected it to be. While in Germany, we were seldom alone. Andy's M.P. duty kept him on base most of the time. When he was home, we were with other Army couples. Reminiscing, I suddenly realized, I had married a stranger who was still a stranger. With a shrug, I dismissed the thought. Andy would be home soon and we would make it work. Determination was my strong point.

Going through customs didn't take long. Standing in line I thought about our future. Before leaving Germany I had received a letter from my uncle of Tujunga, California. He wrote that he and my aunt would be spending a year or so in North Carolina. They wanted Andy and me to live in their furnished three-bedroom home. It would help them and, of course, help us. I concluded that having such an opportunity as this must be a good omen. The marriage would work.

Mom and Dad were waiting at the airport. All the way home we exchanged news. I couldn't get enough. It seemed so long since I'd just talked family talk.

The next day I moved into my aunt and uncle's house. The excitement of having my own home—and such a lovely one— carried me through the six weeks I lived there alone. When Andy arrived home later, freshly discharged from the Army, he was as happy as I to have a home.

Andy went to work for his father whose company did elaborate marble work. I began working part-time in my parents' store.

At first, we had everything going for us, except our marriage relationship. There didn't seem to be anything there. We had never really known one another and when we did take time to get acquainted we found there was absolutely nothing between us. We didn't even like each other - much less love one another.

The differences in our personalities, likes and dislikes, our life-styles were staggering. Andy didn't see things my way—I didn't see them his. He could have made a very good income working for his father on numerous Beverly Hills projects. He enjoyed money and all it could buy but didn't like being committed to a nine-to-five routine. So his workweek usually consisted of whatever he wanted it to be.

In general, Andy and I looked at almost everything differently. I was born to be organized and comfortable with routine. Some of the inconsistencies and uncertainties in our marriage were beginning to get to me. The differences and disagreements erupted into full blown arguments more often than not. I knew this was no way to live, but I wasn't ready to give up.

"Maybe if I get pregnant—-having children might help." It was empty speculation but we did settle our differences long enough for me to get pregnant. We resumed the battling soon after that.

The baby was due July 15, our marriage relationship continued to deteriorate and by the first of June we weren't agreeing on anything. It may have been the constant turmoil that caused our son to be born six weeks prematurely, on June 6. The doctor's prognosis just before his birth was not very promising.

When I was well into labor the doctor shook his head and said, "This baby is too small to survive." As soon as the baby was born a nurse took him and ran. I didn't get to see him or touch him. I thought he was alive but couldn't be sure. For two dreadful hours, no one told me anything. After what seemed an eternity, I was told we had a son and he would probably be all right. He was in an incubator on oxygen because he was not breathing properly. The next twenty-four hours would tell if he were going to live.

I was allowed to see him briefly, slip my hand in the incubator and touch him. So small, so soft, so helpless. He just had to pull through. I knew he would.

In the first few weeks of pregnancy I had experienced some bleeding which prompted the doctor to order me to bed for a few days. I had remembered hearing of all the miscarriages my mother had undergone and hoped this wasn't the beginning of a similar pattern.

Now as I looked at this precious little baby in the incubator, I thought, "I almost lost you at the beginning, and now at birth. But don't give up, little guy. We'll make it. You're going to have a special place in this world."

We named him Dylan Steven. Dylan must have inherited some of his mother's determination, for within a week the problems were solved and we were allowed to take him home.

Dylan's birth was the answer to a lot of things, of course. My days were no longer filled with frustration and turmoil. I saw real purpose in life when caring for this little one. How could anyone be unhappy in the presence of such a happy child? I anticipated a beautiful future for both of us.

Expecting Dylan's birth to cement our marriage, however, was unrealistic, and when our little boy was three months old, Andy and I agreed to divorce. We were already so far apart in our relationship that finalizing it with divorce didn't seem to matter.

* * * * * * *

Chapter Eleven

"I have come as light into the world,
that everyone who believes in Me may not remain in darkness."
John 12:46

D ylan's life started because of my own need.

Thinking back on circumstances surrounding Dylan's birth I realized I had relied on his presence to fill the void created by an unhappy broken marriage. Now, with Rob's death terminating a happy marriage, Dylan had become again the very center of my world. This time, however, I did have the Lord and I could pray for wisdom and understanding.

So the summer before Dylan was to enter fourth grade I reluctantly and prayerfully considered his request to ride his bicycle to school. Three of his friends would be riding bicycles also. Dylan was so responsible. I knew I had to let go sometime.

Two weeks before school began we discussed bicycle riding. We should make proper preparations. So I got in the car and followed Dylan as he made a trial run on his bike to the school ground. I waited for him to place the bike in the rack. Then we both went inside where some of the teachers were getting their rooms ready.

Dylan's teacher was in the fourth grade room and we told him why we had come today. He walked outside with us, explained to Dylan how to lock his bicycle to the rack and the best way to reach that area from the street.

After we arrived back home, we talked about how much we liked the new teacher and how smooth the trial run had been. We discussed bicycle safety rules and I asked Dylan to sit down and make a list of ten rules. He did it carefully and well, and we taped the list to the refrigerator as a constant reminder.

The first day of school it was not planned that the boys would ride their bikes. So I drove Dylan to school that day. Before we left that morning, we prayed together. I gave my son to the Lord and asked that He would watch over Dylan whether he was on the bike or walking or in the car. That He would protect Dylan and give him a really super year and help him to learn a lot.

The boys began to ride together about three times a week. The rest of the time we mothers car-pooled, either because of rain or various school activities.

School began that year on September 9. On Friday, October 9, Dylan and three of his friends rode their bicycles to school. That afternoon, a few minutes after three o'clock, I looked out the window and saw a neighbor running down her driveway and up mine. Something was wrong.

I opened the front door and she yelled, "Dylan's been hit by a car up at the corner."

I grabbed my keys and we jumped in my car and drove to the corner. On the way I kept praying, "God just let it be an arm or a leg. Something we can fix. Please, God, something we can fix."

At the corner we saw a number of vehicles, an ambulance, a fire truck, police car and a trash truck. And people everywhere. Before I could open the car door, another neighbor, a registered nurse, came running up to the car. She had been driving home from work with her son in the car. In front of them they saw an accident involving, not a car, but several trucks, and a form flying in the air. The crumpled bicycle told her the situation was grave. She was the first observer on the scene and, being a trained nurse, she ran immediately to Dylan's lifeless form and began to administer mouth-to-mouth resuscitation. It was useless. The doctor, who came out of the nearby medical center, by some strange quirk, was my family doctor. As they worked together on Dylan, she said, "Dr. Smith, do you know who this is?"

He replied, "No."

She said, "This is Dylan Rasmussen."

Dr. Smith knew it had been less than two years since I had lost my husband. He has since told me that the most difficult thing he ever had to do was to pronounce Dylan dead that day.

The people of the medical profession do have hearts. Mimi, the nurse, proved it when she lost her professional bearing completely and ran up to the car screaming, "He's dead. He's dead. He's dead." She was in shock and I cannot blame her. But that is the harsh way I found out my son was dead. I know now why doctors do not usually treat their own families for serious illness and injury. No one can think professionally and objectively when deeply emotionally involved.

At the time, all I could do was deny it. I said, "No, no, no, no...." Dr. Smith came over and took me into his office. Someone restrained me from going to Dylan. In hysteria, I screamed, "I want my baby. No, no, no!" Dr. Smith gave me a shot and the room became fuzzy around me. I was still repeating over and over, "I want my baby. I want him back."

Finally, I said, "I don't want to be here anymore. I want to go with them."

I realized my parents were in the room, but they seemed far away. My mother was crying and saying, "Dawn's going to die next. Dawn's going to die next." Though not agreeing intentionally, I continued to mumble, "I don't want to be here anymore."

A pastor from our church had arrived and was helping my parents and me into his car. He took us to my parents' home and stayed with us for a while. His kind and gentle presence helped to settle us somewhat. I didn't feel anything. I was numb. That evening I became extremely quiet and didn't talk with anyone. I was in a shell. Or it might more accurately be described as a vacuum.

The next day many people from the church came by. I remember that most of that day I was really distressed. I had the feeling all day that Dylan needed me. That I was his mother and that I was supposed to be taking care of him, and he was somewhere and he was scared and he needed me. I couldn't shake that feeling. I was tormented by it and all day I couldn't get off the subject. I remember telling Bill, a friend from church, "He needs me." I was agitated and a little angry that no one seemed to understand that he needed me. I didn't know what to do about it. Bill patiently listened and then said, "No, Dawn, what you are feeling is not true. Dylan is O.K. He is with Jesus."

Then, about twenty-four hours after those dreadful words, "He's dead" had seared my soul, a sudden peace flooded over me. I was able to say, "This is O.K." The release was not from pain and sorrow, but from the obsessive thought that I had to do something. I knew Dylan really was all right. I knew, also, I had a long way to go before I could say, "I am all right."

The peace that God gave that day carried me through the next few days. The day of the funeral a reporter from the newspaper came to interview me. It wasn't easy to talk about Dylan's death, but even I was surprised at how calmly I spoke. In her human interest story, the reporter said, "When asked how she is able to cope with such pain, Dawn explained she is a 'real strong Christian. . . .The prayers, phone calls, messages and words of consolation are helping her through as they did after her husband's death."

I couldn't bring myself to go home right away after the funeral. So I stayed on with my folks. Someone went to my house and brought back the clothes and other things I needed.

For a month I was on the receiving end of the love and concern of many people. I needed that because I needed to know I was a person. I had not only lost a son, I had lost my identity. I was not a wife. I was not a mother. Who was I? I needed a sense of being, and caring people gave me that.

So many thoughtful things were done, I can't enumerate them all. In a large box of cards, notes and letters, there is a precious consolation card from Dylan's Sunday school class. Sometimes it was hard to see the childish scrawl through the tears. One of the children wrote, "I went to the funeral. It was nice." Another wrote, "I liked Dylan. He was my friend." Those children were so young and were trying to cope with losing a friend so unexpectedly.

Also, in my memory box is a citizenship award that Dylan

received at school. The second week of fourth grade Dylan brought it home. I asked, "What is this for?" He said it was because he had been nice to a new kid, Tommy, and talked to him. No one had been friendly but Dylan had gone up to Tommy and said, "I'll be your friend and show you where everything is." A few days after that, at the school's Open House, I had spoken to Dylan's teacher about the award. He said, "Dylan is a brilliant student and he has a heart of gold."

I recalled the incident after Dylan's death when the principal called to relate another incident. He said that on Friday Dylan had gone in to his teacher and told him what a good week he'd had and how much he liked him.

That was Dylan's way. He liked people and he wasn't afraid to let them know. Remembering those things about him was comforting. But memories cannot fill the void. The road back from darkness to light and living again was long and sometimes very rough.

I knew Dylan was with God, and I knew God was with me. Jesus said, "I will never leave you nor forsake you." I couldn't think further.

* * * * * * *

Chapter Twelve

"Even though I walk through the valley of the shadow of death,
I fear no evil; for Thou art with me..."
Psalm 23:4

*F*riends did so many things for me in those dark days.

Susan called me every day. When I wanted to talk, she was there. When I didn't feel like saying a thing, she understood.

For my friend, Dixie, Dylan's death and my agony opened old wounds. She was always available, though, to share my hurt. Dixie watched and wrote much of what she observed. She shared those notes with me. She had entitled them "With Much Love To My Friend, Dawn." The first entry date was the day of Dylan's death. Sprinkled through this letter of love were words of understanding and encouragement and many scripture promises. I'd like to share her words with you, but my story would be too lengthy and sometimes repetitious. Some of what she wrote I have already said.

Dixie encouraged me to keep my own journal and write down my thoughts—good and bad. It would serve as an emotional release as well as prove helpful later on when I wanted to recall something that might help another. I followed her advice and will share excerpts from my journal. For a long time I didn't want anyone to read these agonizing words. But as I read again the journal in preparation for writing my story, I realized that someone suffering as I had might profit by reading these following thoughts.

On the first page of the journal is a poem from my heart:

MY SON

He came into the world early -
Didn't expect him quite so soon.
A special, happy boy,
Full of love and laughter.

He never knew a stranger.
He touched so many lives.
He always made my proud.
I miss him so.

God took him home early -
I don't understand.
Didn't expect him to go -
Quite so soon.

October 25 (written about the time from October 9 to October 25):

No! No! No! No! No! No! No!

I don't want to be here anymore. I just want to be with Rob and Dylan. I want him back! I want him back.

Dylan! Dylan! Dylan! No...

I felt he was somewhere that he needed me. I wanted to help him but didn't know how. The mother part of me wanted to help him somehow, some way. Is he afraid? Is he crying? I can't stand it. He was always so worried about me and my feelings. Can he see me hurting? I don't want him to be unhappy.

On Sunday some kind of release seemed to come of the feeling that he needed me. I felt that he was truly with the Lord and O.K.

Who needs me? No purpose anymore. I went home today and went into Dylan's room. I was hoping this would bring a slap of reality. He is really gone. But I just seem to be so calm like nothing has happened. I don't understand. Why am I not crying all the time? Is it denial or shock? The funeral and seeing him at the chapel all seems like a dream. I can't believe that Dylan actually is buried (body, not spirit).

I have a dream that someone is telling me over and over that he is dead. I say, "No, he's not, he just has a headache and he'll be fine!" I seem to be going through the motions. I am numb. It's a nightmare and I'll wake up. He's not really dead.

I seem to feel his presence, or maybe it's God's presence with me. I don't feel alone now.

I don't remember the first few weeks when Rob died. It seems like I was in a trance of some kind. I remember thinking that because I was a Christian I was just supposed to accept it. The anger came out months later—at Rob and God. After that, I really began to grieve, cried a lot. Dylan was always by my side when he heard me, patting my shoulder. (Sometimes I think I feel him there now.) I know I felt a little better reading about the stages of the grief process and identifying with them. I was always wondering if what I was feeling was NORMAL. The books people have given me helped me to feel I was.

I felt a victory within over time. I noticed I was progressing through the stages. I anticipated the one-year mark. Thought I would feel better and I did.

I know how BAD the first year was and I am really afraid of trying to do it again—ALONE (humanly).

I can't seem to pray much, don't know what to say, just bits and pieces of promises and scripture.

I keep thinking of Romans 8:28: "And we know that God causes ALL THINGS to work together for good to those who love God…"

I can believe that but I can't believe Dylan is dead. Seems like Rob is, but not Dylan. Will acceptance come bit by bit or just hit me hard?

I'm tired all the time, don't care if I do anything, but I do feel better if someone takes me out somewhere. Hard to make decisions about anything, even dumb simple questions.

I want to see him, but can't seem to, even when I look at his pictures and sit in his room. I think it will come later.

October 29

Yesterday I began to get mad. Mad at God for doing this to me AGAIN. I thought I was doing a good job and I grew and witnessed a lot after my husband died. I was studying my Bible every day, going to church, Bible study, working on the bulletin, being a good witness and then MY SON DIED! What does the Lord want of me? Why another slap when I was trying so hard? I felt when Rob died, God used that to teach me to be better but now it just makes me mad that he would take Dylan too. What more does he want of me? What should I have been doing differently?

October 30

My anger seemed to drain out of me today and peace returned. It's my birthday and some girls are having a luncheon for me. Tonight some other girls are taking me to dinner and a movie. I feel sick to my stomach, can't imagine how I'll eat both times. (I went

and it felt better to be cared about and be with my friends.)
<u>November 2</u>

Last night I had a dream. I dreamed I was working through the church somehow with a group helping people who were lonely and grieving, some knew the Lord and some didn't. It was like a revelation to me from God. He was telling me there was a job to do right here in this town. I don't have to be a missionary in a foreign country. I can do so much right here. When I woke up from the dream, I felt good.

* * * * * * *

Chapter Thirteen

"Now we see in a mirror dimly, but then face to face;
now I know in part, but then I shall know fully
just as I also have been fully known."
I Corinthians 13:12

I *knew there were stages of grief.*

Recalling some of the things I had read about grief after Rob died, I tried desperately to move from one stage of grief to the next. I soon discovered that while there may be a general pattern, it is never a cut-and-dried process.

The initial stages of shock and denial I had experienced is common to most people who have lost a loved one, particularly if the death was unexpected and violent. Now there should be no more denial, but a time of bargaining, or a time of anger. All of these emotions are normal, but I found myself see-sawing back and forth, from one to the other. Depression came and went. Would the despair always be there? Was I ever to function again as a normal human being?

Thinking back on those times, as I look again to my journal, I see what an emotional roller coaster I was on. Only God could straighten my path. Only God had the answers I was seeking.

As the journal reveals, it took over a year for life to begin having meaning again. It seemed an interminable length of time to me. To the God of eternity, time is not measured...nor wasted. He was patiently helping me to grow closer to Him, to understand more fully the truths he was teaching me.

Excerpts from the rest of my journal are reproduced below. They truly speak the language of my heart during the fourteen months following my son's death.

November 6

The 4ᵗʰ of November was Rob's birthday. It really didn't bother me this year. Tonight I am home, going to spend the night here for the first time since Dylan died. I don't want any company, want to be alone. I still just can't believe that he's dead. It doesn't seem real to me.

November 7

Last night I thought I would wash some clothes, but when I opened the hamper all I could do was cry. The more of Dylan's clothes I picked up the harder I cried. It was what I had wanted to do for a while (cry). But I don't feel any better today for it. Today I am just depressed.

November 8

So far I'm not scared to be here alone. I'm thankful for that as I think it is important to adjust here alone. I felt better after going to church today.

November 9

Last night when I went to bed, I got really upset and cried really hard. I kept saying, "It hurts, God," over and over. I was down and depressed all day today. Still wondering, "Why Dylan and why me, again?"

November 14

The same thoughts have been going through my head for the last few days. Did God cause this or only allow it? Is it my fault because I let him ride the bike? Maybe I'm looking for someone to blame. I want to understand.

November 16

I can accept Dylan's death if it was God's will, but if He only allowed it to happen, then could it have been prevented and am I the one who could have prevented it? (Guilt)

(With Rob I blamed him for going out that night. I knew I needed to forgive him but I also knew that God could have saved him if He wanted to. So the final blame would have to be on God and I didn't want to be mad at Him as I knew I would only end up bitter and never find peace.)

November 18

I went to Bible study today and the speaker talked about how when you feel irrational guilt that Satan is the accuser. It is a lie from Satan that you are being punished for being a bad person when tragedy comes. God does not work that way. He is a God of love and grace. I am beginning to feel that it doesn't matter why the accident happened. I was a good mother and I couldn't be expected to keep a fourth grader off a bicycle. It is wrong for me to go through life blaming myself. I did everything I could possibly think of to protect Dylan. It happened. God will see me through.

December 2

Sometimes when I get to thinking about Dylan I just can't stand it. Not being able to see him, hear him and hug him. I get so scared that I just can't take this. It's so quiet here!

December 6

I feel a terrible loss but I also feel God's grace and strength helping me. I know he is uplifting me and carrying me through. I could not make it without Him.

December 9

Today has been two years since Rob died and two months since Dylan died. It doesn't seem like two years since Rob was here and it doesn't even seem real to me that Dylan is gone. I always have more trouble anticipating the anniversary dates then when they actually get here. I was so upset all day yesterday and last night that by the time this morning came I was already exhausted, and the worst was over.

December 10

The Kupstas family from church lost their 17-year-old boy, Dwayne, in a car accident today. I didn't really know them but I wanted to go and tell them I care and I understand. I don't know if it helped them or not but I felt better by reaching out to them.

December 14

Dwayne's funeral was today at my church. I was comforted about Dylan from what the pastors said about eternal life. It gave me the feeling that Dylan really didn't die at all; he is just living in a place now where I can't be with him. Someday we'll be together forever. I'm thankful that I am a Christian so I have that assurance of seeing him again. That hope is what keeps me going. I told everybody that I sent Christmas cards to this year of that assurance.

December 17

Today I woke up crying. I cried all day. I just miss Dylan so much I can't stand it and Christmas is really affecting me. I miss Rob, too. I feel so lost and alone.

December 19

Yesterday and today I have been depressed and mad. I don't understand why I have to lose everything. It's just not fair. I'm so tired of struggling and I want my son back. I opened a Christmas card from Dylan's Sunday school class and I wanted his name to be on there and someone else's gone. I wanted him to have signed that card for some other mother. (Resentment) I feel sick to my stomach and so tired.

December 24

I came to Sunland for Christmas, couldn't imagine staying home by myself. I've been having a bad day today, seeing all the kids. They are so excited and I knew what Dylan would be like if he were here right now. I wish Christmas were over.

January 4

Home again and today when I woke up there was about ten inches of snow on the ground and it made me miss Dylan so much.

He loved the snow and he should be here playing in it. It's just not fair. I cried for him and for me. I had thought that when the new year got here I would feel better, but I don't. I was supposed to start work today but I can't get the car out and the power is out.

January 10

I started school on the 7th. Tomorrow I start back to work. Maybe the routine will help me to feel better. I need some purpose to my life, I think. I don't know who I am or what I want out of life, but most of the time I really don't care. I lost my identity, as I am not a wife or a mother anymore. I really don't know who Dawn is.

January 17

It has been good to be back at work. I feel more needed and important doing my job. It bothered me the first day to get off work and realize I had to go home alone. No one was waiting for me anywhere.

January 24

Last night I began to take down all the things off Dylan's bedroom walls. The room looks so awful, so empty. I took off the headboard that said "DYLAN" and changed the sheets. Tonight I walked in there and picked up his bedspread and finally really let loose. It hit me that I have to let him go and I don't know if I can. It hurts so much. I miss him and love him and I don't want to give him up. I finally cried tonight with big, heaving sobs. And no one to pat me on the shoulder.

March 10

Most of the last month has been full of anger, guilt and depression. Self-pity has been with me almost continually. I've had an obsession about dying. I've had dreams that I was dying. I've missed Dylan so much that I just cried all day; it hurt so badly. I have finally decided that there is no right or wrong way to grieve. As long as you don't just pretend it didn't happen completely. Everyone grieves differently. Some people cry every day, some occasionally after it builds up. Some people clean out the person's room immediately and some wait a few months.

Most people are afraid of not being normal at this time, but really there is no normal for everyone. I try to remember it will pass, grief doesn't come to stay, it comes to pass. Even when I don't believe it, I try to remember it. It has been real hard for me lately to listen to other people talk about their kids. I really feel put out when people think that I'd want to hear what so and so said and did. I guess resentment goes hand in hand with self-pity.

March 11

Sometimes I feel such peace and I feel so close to God that it really is O.K. That Rob and Dylan died. I have grown so much; He has been with me and taught me so much. I never would know God this way if it weren't for the tragedies in my life.

April 11

It's Easter Sunday. It's hard. I want Dylan to be here to have an Easter basket and look for Easter eggs, to laugh and smile and say, "I love you, Mom."

<u>May 5</u>

The last two weeks have just been awful. I've been depressed about Mother's Day coming, then Dylan's birthday. The Women's Single Group I've been meeting with is having a barbecue in the park and you are supposed to bring your children. My Sunday school class is doing four weeks on interpersonal (marriage) relationships and then four weeks on raising children. I don't feel like I fit anywhere.

I went to see my pastor today. At first he made me mad because he said it sounded like I created a lot of my own problems. I told him I just didn't feel like praying or reading the Word. By the time I left his office I realized that he was right and I needed to hear what he said. God is the only answer no matter what the problem. I need to keep my eyes on Him and not the problems.

<u>June 6</u>

Today would have been Dylan's tenth birthday. I have been so down and depressed anticipating this day. So have my parents. When I woke up this morning I didn't feel alone. I felt very comforted and had a real peace. When I got to church and saw my Mom and Dad I could sense that they felt that way, too. So many people are praying for us today and I can feel it.

<u>June 24</u>

Sheba, that was Dylan's cat, was killed today. It makes me so angry. I can't even have a cat! I feel like everything is taken away from me. I guess my anger is mainly directed at God. I feel that if all I can have to love in this world is two cats, then why can't He at least protect them!

July 26

Last week I got hired at the hospital and today is my first day of training. I feel as if the Lord gave me this job.

August 27

Today my girlfriend, Susie, died of cancer. She has been fighting this battle for three years. I feel relieved more than anything that she won't have to suffer anymore. I know she is with the Lord now and part of me really envied her. I honestly think she is better off than we are here in this crummy world.

September 7

I have had some really bad days the last two weeks. I have been down and missed Dylan so much. I wanted him to go in to the fifth grade with all the other kids tomorrow. I knew it didn't make sense but I couldn't help it. Finally, within the past couple of days I've got my eyes back on the Lord in my life. The inner peace that I feel within when I stay in fellowship with the Lord is so amazing and so complete.

October 9

One year ago today my son died. I feel a little nauseated. My heart has been breaking the past three days.

November 14

The past week or so I haven't been able to hold on to the peace and comfort I know the Lord can give me. I'm full of questions again. I want to be a good witness for the Lord but I'm tired of feel-

ing bad and I don't feel like I'm offering anything. It's hard to care about everyday life and going to work and Bible study. I just like being home alone. Lately I've been wondering if there really is a God and will I really see Rob and Dylan again? Is Satan trying to destroy my faith? Where is God?

December 30

I had a good Christmas with my Mom and Dad, my brother Dick and sister-in-law Betty, and my two nieces, Sharon and Debbie. It was the first Christmas in about five years that everyone was healthy and it was so nice. I missed Dylan and Rob but I was full of peace and so thankful to be with my family.

A couple of days after Christmas I suddenly figured out that everyone does have a "time to die." I always wondered if Rob hadn't been out that night or Dylan hadn't been on the bike would they have died anyway? How could they have died if say—they were at home? I realized that they could have been sick for days or months or even years with cancer and still have died at that same time. Rob could have been home doing some work and have gotten electrocuted or fallen in the shower, or off the roof. Our days are numbered and God who knows the number of hairs on our heads is in complete control. (Psalm 139:16 "You saw me before I was born and scheduled each day of my life before I began to breathe. Every day was recorded in your book.") *What a relief to finally stop saying, "What if, what if." This is all part of God's plan.*

* * * * * * * *

Chapter 14

"Blessed are those who mourn, for they shall be comforted."
Matthew 5:4

I read in Psalms that God has a plan for everyone before he is born.

God surely knew when my parents named me "Dawn" that there would be much darkness in my life. Each time I have groped my way out into the light of God's presence I discovered I was never really alone. God was always there. Even when my numbed senses said, "No, there is no hope," He knew how I hurt and He cared.

I'm learning not to trust my feelings—sometimes I don't "feel" God's presence. I must trust what I know to be true. God is present. God loves me. I am never alone—not ever—no matter how lonely I may feel.

In the book of Isaiah God has promised, *"...beauty for ashes, joy instead of mourning, praise instead of heaviness."*

I pray that God will use me to help someone else who is sorrowing or struggling. When I think about it, I know He did begin answering that prayer before I had formulated it in my own heart. First with Susan as she was drawn to become a Christian after Rob's death.

Next, in an established friendship with Linnea. After her son,

Patrick, was born, she returned to Cape Cod where she lived for three years. Through letters and telephone calls we periodically shared our emotional highs and lows. Linnea's heart ached for me after Dylan's death. It was especially difficult for her to handle because she suddenly felt exposed and vulnerable. Just as Susan and I had once concluded, she, too, thought she was safe from any more loss after her husband's death. She had "paid her dues" so to speak. We had many long talks and our friendship was an encouragement to both of us. After three years, Linnea sold her house in Cape Cod and returned to Paradise. She is now an active member of our church's singles' group, opening her home for our Thursday night Bible studies.

Then there was Lee, Susan's father. He was dying of cancer. He had decided that since he had lived a lifetime without acknowledging the Lord, it was too late now. He had a strong sense of justice and didn't think it was fair to turn to God now. He didn't see how I could cope. We became friends and I shared with him how God had been my strength. I told him how I had come to know the Lord. I also told him it is never too late to turn to God.

One day, when he was very ill, I sat on the side of his bed talking with him. He listened intently. I gave him a small picture of Sallman's painting of Christ standing at the door knocking. I said, "That door represents the entrance to your heart, or life. You know He is there. But unless you open that door, it's no use. He won't come in and you won't get to Heaven." Revelation 3:20 reads, *"Behold, I stand at the door and knock; if anyone hears My voice and opens the door, I will come in to him, and will dine with him, and he with Me."* Lee didn't respond but he didn't seem angry and I knew he was seriously thinking over what I had said. He knew he didn't have long to live.

When I got home, I wrote him a letter telling him that before he died, Susan had to know he was going to Heaven. I doubt if he would have accepted such a blunt letter from most people, but we had established an open communication, and I felt compelled to write. I had been witnessing and sharing and was certain he would accept the Lord. I had gone through losing Rob and not knowing. I didn't want Susan to have to go through the rest of her life wondering if her father had made that decision. So I wrote, "Look, she has to know."

Shortly after that Lee told Susan of my letter. He wanted to reassure me. He said, "I know I am no longer alone and I am going to Heaven." He said he asked forgiveness of his sins and he asked the Lord to come in and take over his life. He said he felt a peace come over him at that instant and the fear was gone. He knew he was no longer alone and was positive he was going to Heaven.

One month later he died.

"Misery loves company," isn't just a funny little saying. There is a deeper meaning that I have discovered. When one is sorrowful and suffering, there is a longing to talk with someone who understands, someone who has experienced the same suffering.

I believe, ultimately, God wants each of us to experience His presence in those times. To know that Jesus Christ suffered every hurt and knows exactly how we feel. He has been there and He takes us through every difficult valley. Along the way, however, God has also graciously allowed us to draw comfort and consolation from one another.

Not long ago, I received a telephone call from a friend, Keith. Keith and his family had been members of our church before moving to another city. Soon after the move their little five-year-old daughter, Lori, was diagnosed as having bone cancer. Our entire church family had prayed for Lori as she underwent a series of surgeries and painful treatments. Finally, after two years God mercifully took her back home to be with Him. Keith and his wife, Debi, are Christians. They know Lori is all right now. They are just beginning to walk that same sorrowful road I did from darkness to light. There is no easy way.

Keith confided that even though his heart was breaking he hadn't been able to cry. Debi cried all the time. He wanted to dispose of all of Lori's things. Debi wanted to keep everything. I could identify with both of them. I had been there.

As I have already said, there is a general pattern of grief which most people seem to follow more or less in progressive stages: shock, denial, anger, guilt, depression, acceptance, and growth. Each of us spends different lengths of time in each stage. Sometimes the stages overlap. Sometimes our emotions do repeat performances moving from guilt to anger to guilt. We should never try to fit another into our mold, even in grief. As I wrote in the journal, there is no normal way to grieve. What is normal? Each person is different. Because God made each of us unique, we must allow for differences. In grief that is shared, as with a father and mother who have lost a child, we can't expect that each will have the same emotions at the same time.

After Lori's death, I was asked to speak to the Marriage and Family Sunday School class to which Keith and Debi had belonged. The class wanted some input on how they could best help their bereaved friends. What do you say to a parent who has lost a child? How can you help?

I suggested:

1. Talk to Debi and Keith—don't avoid them because you don't know what to say. Say you care, say, "I'm praying." Don't say you understand if you haven't been there, because they know you don't. Be available, give them a hug.

2. Let them talk about Lori—you can't just pretend she didn't exist. It is important and necessary for them to talk about her. It's healing. So listen and don't change the subject.

3. Remember them a few months after the funeral— that is when reality sets in. Holidays are terrible and this Christmas will be hardest.

4. You call or help if you see a need—a grieving person doesn't want to impose on anyone or bother others.

5. It's O.K. to cry—it is not a sign of lack of faith. God gave us tears to release emotion.

6. Keep them in prayer—as often as the Lord
   brings them to your mind.

My closing prayer that day was, "Dear Heavenly Father, help Debi and Keith to hang on tightly to your hand as You take them through the deep waters."

* * * * * * *

Chapter Fifteen

*"...who comforts us in all our affliction so that we may be able to
comfort those who are in any affliction with the comfort
with which we ourselves are comforted by God."*
II Corinthians 1:4

I often have an opportunity to share experiences with individuals.

Occasionally, I am asked to speak to a larger group. I always pray for God's words and God's wisdom and that God will be glorified. I can only say what God has shown me. He is the source of all good and if He chooses to make some good come out of my sorrow, I will praise Him for it.

The first time I was asked to speak publicly was at an Easter cantata at the church. They said, "Would you just tell your story?" I was not sure, "Tell my story? Why? Surely there are lots of other people out there with sad stories. I'm only one person. The world is full of hurting people. Why should I tell my story?"

They answered, "Because there are so many hurting people. You have experienced God's comfort and hope in each crisis. Some don't have that hope, you know."

I agreed. A crisis without Christ is to be hopeless as well as helpless. It's a meaningless existence. I could so easily have been there, but God lifted me out of the dark into the light.

I don't know what God has in store for me. The most recent involvement of ministry in my life has been with the singles in our church. There are so many hurting people in this segment of our society. It is also an area of need that is often neglected. I find it helpful in relating to singles that I have been where most of them are. For those who have never married, the divorced single parent, the widow, and the widowed single parent, and the bereaved parent who has lost a child, I really can say, "I understand." I have been there, too.

A minister to singles said recently, "Dawn, because of what you have experienced, God has given you a license to minister to those who hurt." He may be right, but I believe that every Christian who cares about others also has that license. We have just been given different tools. I can identify because I, too, have suffered. Someone else may help just by being available, by allowing the love of Christ to work through him or her.

I don't want anything that has happened to me to be wasted in God's scheme of things. I know Rob and Dylan lived for a reason, and died for a reason. God knows why. I don't have to know.

So I can say: "I am thankful for all that has happened to me."

"I am thankful for my first marriage because through it I was given a son."

"I am thankful for the second marriage because I experienced what it was like to be really in love and to be loved."

"I can be thankful for Dylan because I know the love of a mother and a son."

Some of the things God allowed in my life may not have been in His perfect plan for me because he allowed me to make mistakes when I acted in my will, not His. But I see His hand has been in it all to bring me to where I am now.

I have settled on this:

"In good times and in bad times, God is there and God is enough."

* * * * * * *

Epilogue

After being divorced, then widowed, then losing my son, I was unwilling to really get involved in another relationship. I didn't date at all for over five years. I was comfortable being on my own and kept busy by working full time and serving at my church. I was complete in knowing that God was all I truly needed.

One Sunday I met a visitor named "Wally" at church. He had been through his own "hard times" and was new to the Singles Sunday school class. He was a kind, gentle man with a true servant's heart. As he and I became involved in leadership of the Singles ministry, the Lord was drawing us together.

We began to date and little by little I let Wally in and he slowly broke through the wall I had around my heart. Wally proposed once and I said, "no." He proposed again and I said, "no." Then one night as I was reading the Word and praying I suddenly knew that God was telling me that the next time Wally proposed my answer should be, "yes!" Boy was Wally surprised!

God has truly blessed us with a wonderful marriage and we continue serving Him still at the Christian and Missionary Alliance Church in Paradise, California.

Printed in the United States
16085LVS00001B/7-195